NORMAN
PRICE

BELLA
LASAGNE

JAMES

SARAH

MEET ALL THESE FRIENDS IN BUZZ BOOKS:

Thomas the Tank Engine
The Animals of Farthing Wood
Biker Mice From Mars
Winnie-the-Pooh
Fireman Sam
Rupert
Babar

First published in Great Britain 1990 by Buzz Books
an imprint of Reed Children's Books
Michelin House, 81 Fulham Road, London SW3 6RB
and Auckland, Melbourne, Singapore and Toronto
Reprinted 1992 and 1994

Fireman Sam copyright © 1985 Prism Art & Design Limited
Text and illustrations copyright © 1990 Reed International Books Limited
Story by Caroline Hill-Trevor
Illustrations by CLIC!
Based on the animation series produced by Bumper Films for
S4C/Channel 4 Wales and Prism Art & Design Limited
Original idea by Dave Gingell and Dave Jones, assisted by Mike Young
Characters created by Rob Lee
All rights reserved

ISBN 1 85591 032 2

Printed and bound in Italy by Olivotto

ELVIS'S
EXPERIMENT

Story by Caroline Hill-Trevor
Illustrations by CLIC!

Firefighter Elvis Cridlington and Fireman
Sam were on their way back to Pontypandy
after a fire. "Let's hope that's it for today,
Fireman Sam," said Elvis as they drove into
Pontypandy. "Penny Morris is coming over
from Newtown for supper and I'm going to
cook something extra special."

"Your cooking is always extra special, or
extra-ordinary!" said Fireman Sam
laughing. "What's it tonight, Elvis?"

"Just you wait. When they hear about tonight, the Newtown brigade will wish I was their cook," said Elvis.

"And so will the Pontypandy brigade!" laughed Fireman Sam, as Jupiter drew up outside his house. "Could you drop me here please? I'd better change if we've got company tonight. I'll see you later."

"Humph," thought Elvis as he drove on towards the fire station. "I'll make Fireman Sam eat his words, if he's got room that is. I'm going to cook something that's really delicious, and very healthy. But what?" Then suddenly he had a brainwave. "Got it!" he shouted out loud.

8

"The perfect food. I'll show Fireman Sam just how good a cook I really am." Elvis parked Jupiter in the station and ran inside. "There'll be plenty of time to tidy up later," he said to himself. But Elvis was so pleased with his idea he completely forgot to refill Jupiter's water tank.

First Elvis made a big salad and then he started on his experiment. Nut cutlets, but with a difference!

"I bet Penny's never had deep fried nut cutlets before," he said, smiling as he poured the oil into the pan. "She's going to be so impressed."

"Gosh, Elvis, these cutlets are really something," she'd say. "You're the best cook in the valley!" And Elvis blushed at the thought.

In a daydream, Elvis chopped up the nuts and made twelve perfect cutlets. It took him ages. "There now, there's just time to change before Penny arrives," he said, as he put them carefully into the fryer.

Then suddenly he remembered that he
had to clean Jupiter for Station Officer
Steele's inspection. "Oh my!" he flapped,
grabbing a bucket and cloth and dashing
out of the kitchen.

"Who says you can't be a firefighter and a cook," Elvis said to himself as he set to work. But he was so busy polishing Jupiter that he completely forgot about his experiment. "Penny's going to be able to see her face in Jupiter," he said, humming gleefully to himself.

Elvis was woken from his daydream by
the sound of a siren. "That's funny," said
Elvis, looking up. "I wonder what's going
on." The sound came closer and closer until
it stopped right outside the fire station! Elvis
looked out of the window and saw
Firefighter Penny Morris's rescue tender
parked outside.

Elvis scrambled out of Jupiter.

"Evenin', Penny," he said. "You must be hungry. You arrived in such a hurry anyone would think you've come to put out a fire!"

Fireman Sam came running up.

16

"Gracious," gasped Elvis. "Everyone's early tonight. Well I'm afraid you'll have to wait a while for your supper – but it'll be worth it, believe me!"

Fireman Sam and Penny looked at each other, then back at Elvis.

"But we *have* come to put out a fire, Elvis,"
cried Penny.

"Really Elvis, you're meant to be a
firefighter and you don't even notice a
fire when it's right here, under your nose!"

18

said Fireman Sam. And then he added,
"Surely even you must have noticed the
smell of burning nuts!"

"Burning nuts," murmured Elvis, going
pale. "I'd better get the hose."

Quickly Elvis pulled out the hose.

Nothing happened. "It must be blocked," shouted Fireman Sam. "You did refill the tank, didn't you, Elvis?"

"Oh no, now I'm in trouble," groaned Elvis, going even paler.

"We don't want the hose, anyway," said
Penny. "We need a fire extinguisher for
this." And she took one out of the rescue
tender. "I always carry this in case of
emergencies," she explained.

"Thank you, Firefighter Morris," said Fireman Sam, taking the extinguisher. He pulled on his mask and went into the kitchen.

"I wonder what caused the fire, don't you, Elvis?" asked Penny.

"Um," stuttered Elvis, trembling.

"What's going on here?" said Station Officer Steele, arriving at the fire station. "This is only an experimental exercise, I presume?"

"Sort of, you could say," replied Elvis, going bright red.

"Fire's out. Not much damage done," said
Fireman Sam, coming outside again. "But
I'm afraid whatever you were frying is
ruined, Elvis."

24

"Frying!" bellowed Station Officer Steele.
"But I thought I'd banned fried food, on
Firefighter Morris's advice. Too much fat
isn't good for you, is it?"

"But . . ." stammered Elvis.

"That's right, Sir, it's better not to eat too much fried food," agreed Penny.

"But I was cooking nut cutlets, deep fried, as an experiment. I thought they'd be

tastier that way," explained Elvis, looking
sorry for himself. "However hard I try,
something always goes wrong."

"Or someone always goes wrong,"
laughed Fireman Sam.

"Cheer up, Elvis, let's go to Bella's café and have pasta instead!"

"Yummy," said Elvis smiling again. "That sound's delicious, and even better, I don't have to do the cooking. Making all those cutlets was driving me nuts!"

FIREMAN SAM

STATION OFFICER STEELE

TREVOR EVANS

ELVIS CRIDLINGTON

PENNY MORRIS